Too Many Treasures

backpack mysteries

9705

a backpack Mystery

Too Many Treasures

Mary Carpenter reid

BETHANY HOUSE PUBLISHERS
MINNEAPOLIS, MINNESOTA 55438

Too Many Treasures
Copyright © 1996
Mary Carpenter Reid

Cover and story illustrations by Paul Turnbaugh.

Published by Bethany House Publishers
A Ministry of Bethany Fellowship International
11400 Hampshire Avenue South
Bloomington, Minnesota 55438

Printed in the United States of America by
Bethany Press International, Bloomington, Minnesota, 55438

Library of Congress Cataloging-in-Publication Data

Reid, Mary.
    Too many treasures / Mary Carpenter Reid.
        p.   cm. — (A Backpack mystery ; 1)
    Summary: While staying with their aunt, Steff and her younger sister Paulie discover that someone really is after the valuable old clock that Aunt Opal keeps hidden amid all the other stuff that is crammed into her house.
    ISBN 1–55661–715–1
    [1. Mystery and detective stories. 2. Aunts—Fiction. 3. Orderliness—Fiction. 4. Christian life—Fiction.] I. Title. II. Series: Reid, Mary. Backpack mystery ; 1.
PZ7.R2727To   1996
[Fic]—dc20
96–25234
                                                          CIP
                                                          AC

To Katie—
a favorite person
in my family.

MARY CARPENTER REID loves to visit places just like the places Steff and Paulie visit. Does she stay with peculiar relatives? That's her secret!

She will tell you her family is wonderful. She likes reading and writing children's books. She likes colors and computers. She especially likes getting letters from her readers.

She can't organize things as well as Steff does, but she makes lots of lists.

Two cats—a calico cat and a tiger cat—live at her house in California. *They* are very peculiar!

contents

Do not store up for yourselves treasures on earth.

Matthew 6:19

back door prowler

Steff Larson wished it was not so dark and foggy.

She could barely see Aunt Opal's house from the sidewalk.

"Come on, Paulie," she told her younger sister. "Help me bring our bags."

Paulie didn't move. "It's creepy here."

"It is not creepy," said Steff. "It's foggy because we are near the ocean."

Suddenly, a car horn blasted.

Paulie yelped.

A teenage boy in the car yelled, "Hey, Steff! I can't sit here in the middle of the street with the motor running all night. I'm leaving."

Steff yelled back, "Don't you dare leave yet! My mom is paying you to wait until Paulie and I get inside my aunt's house."

SCR-E-E-E-CH! A van jerked to a stop behind the car, then squeezed past it.

"I'm blocking traffic," the teenager called. "Gotta go!"

Steff warned, "I'm telling my mom not to pay you."

"She already did." The car sped away.

Steff shouted down the street, "I'm telling her anyway. And I'll tell your mother, too."

She turned to Paulie. "When we get home, I'll walk over to his house. I will tell his mother that he drove off and left us standing here in the dark."

Paulie tugged at the straps on her backpack and looked at the sidewalk. Her voice wobbled. "I wish Mom could have brought us."

Steff wished the same thing.

But she said, "Well, Mom couldn't. Don't

worry. We stayed here with Aunt Opal once before."

"Only for two nights," Paulie said. "This is for a lot of nights. Aunt Opal is so . . . so . . . you know."

"Yes. But we can't stand out here."

The house looked awfully dark. Steff began to wonder if Aunt Opal was home.

"She probably doesn't want us," Paulie whispered.

"She told Mom we could come, didn't she?"

"I hope Mom let her know how tall I am now. I don't want to sleep on a cot like I did the other time."

"Sleeping on a cot didn't hurt you."

"It's okay for you to talk," Paulie said. "You had a whole couch to yourself. Try sleeping on a cot with hundreds of packages of yarn."

"Aunt Opal has probably knitted that into something by now," Steff said. "Anyway, she told Mom we'd have bunk beds."

The porch was crowded with a round table and two chairs. Flowerpots lined the porch railing. A pile of driftwood filled one corner.

Suddenly, the curtains on the round window in the front door parted.

A thin face with glasses peered out. It was Aunt Opal. She looked like a picture in a round frame.

Aunt Opal jerked open the door. The puff of gray hair on top of her head flopped this way and that.

"Come in quickly. Hurry." She hustled the girls inside and slammed the door.

The living room was even more crowded than Steff remembered. They followed Aunt Opal on a path between high stacks of boxes and bundles.

Little statues perched everywhere. Bunches of dried flowers covered the top of the piano. There were lots of newspapers.

Aunt Opal stopped often. She seemed to be looking for something.

The girls followed her into the kitchen.

Cereal boxes sat in a row on the table, like books on a shelf.

"Oh, good," Paulie whispered to Steff. "Cocoa Crunches."

Aunt Opal opened a cabinet door. A spice can tumbled out.

"Get that, will you, dear?" Aunt Opal said.

Steff did, but she couldn't fit the spice can back in the cabinet. She turned to find another place. Her backpack swung across the counter and tipped over a basket of oranges. Steff picked them up and asked, "Could we please put our backpacks on our beds?"

"Beds?" Aunt Opal still seemed to be looking for something.

Paulie leaned close to Steff and muttered, "I knew it. I have to sleep with the yarn."

Aunt Opal stood on tiptoe and peered on top of the icebox.

"Did you lose something, Aunt Opal?" Steff asked politely.

"Goodness, no. I never lose anything."

Aunt Opal pushed a wisp of gray hair back into the puff on top of her head. She peeked into the oven.

Steff peeked in, too. "There's nothing in the oven."

"Of course not," Aunt Opal said. "Looking

in the oven is just a trick. I am staying away from my real hiding places. I don't want to show him where I hide my treasure."

"Who's 'him'?" asked Steff.

"What treasure?" asked Paulie.

Aunt Opal rolled her eyes toward a window in the back door. There was no shade on that window.

Aunt Opal whispered, "He may be out there watching."

Paulie gasped.

Steff's stomach did a flip-flop. "Wh-who might be watching?"

Aunt Opal reached into a cabinet. She moved bags of potato chips around.

"Why, my dear, the prowl . . ."

The bags made rustling noises. Steff wasn't quite sure what Aunt Opal said.

She gulped. "Did you say, *PROWLER?*"

Paulie grabbed Steff's arm and whispered, "I told you it was creepy here."

2

ʃoda caN trap

Aunt Opal said, "While I was gone today, someone sneaked into my house."

"Oooh," said Paulie. "To steal your money?"

"No, not money." Aunt Opal picked up a cookie jar that looked like a chicken. "He wants my treasure."

"Is that your treasure?" Paulie asked.

"Oh no. Only money and cookies in here." Aunt Opal took off the lid. She popped a cookie into her mouth. "Help yourself."

The girls each ate a cookie.

They took another and another.

Finally, Steff reached in for a cookie and pulled out a dollar bill.

"Oops," said Aunt Opal.

Just then, a loud crash sounded outside the kitchen door.

CLATTER—CLANG—BANG!

Paulie squealed. Her mouth was full of cookie. Crumbs sprayed all over.

The noise went on and on, like a hundred spoons beating on a hundred metal pans.

Then came a long cry. *YE-OO-OOW!*

Steff wanted to run.

Aunt Opal crept to the door and peeked out. "The rascal is gone."

"Was that a cat?" Steff asked hopefully.

Aunt Opal shook her head. "No. It was that snoopy prowler. But I was ready for him this time."

"I wish it was a cat," Paulie said.

Aunt Opal grinned. "He fell into my trap. That'll teach him."

"What trap?" asked Steff.

"I stacked soda cans on the back porch. He knocked them over."

Steff looked outside. Soda cans lay all around, like splashes of silver in the dark.

Paulie said, "Oh, Aunt Opal! Now the prowler has seen your money in the cookie jar."

But Aunt Opal didn't seem to care. She said, "I must help you girls put your things in your bedroom. Come on."

She led the way past several doors before she opened one.

Paulie cried, "Bunk beds! With nothing stacked on them. Oh, thank you, Aunt Opal."

"They are beautiful," Steff said.

The girls got ready for bed.

Except for the bunk beds and a little space in the middle, the room was very crowded.

Steff did not like clutter. She wanted things to be in their proper places. She liked things to be organized. She liked to keep records, too, and write down plans.

That's why she wanted a planner. Not just a simple planning notebook. She wanted a real planning *system*.

The system she wanted would look like a small book. It would have a real leather cover and a special calendar. Special little books and papers would fit inside. There would be a special pen. But planning systems cost a lot of money.

Paulie climbed to the top bunk. "Steff, what if the prowler comes back?"

Steff snorted. "What prowler? I think a cat knocked over those soda cans."

Paulie's voice got wobbly again. "But Aunt Opal said a prowler sneaked into this house today."

"Now, Paulie," Steff said. "Do you really think Aunt Opal could be sure someone was inside her house?"

"But she told us. . . ."

Steff raised her eyebrows. "This house is so neat and all."

"Oh, yeah." Paulie giggled. "I didn't think of that."

Steff giggled, too. She didn't want Paulie to be frightened. Steff turned out the light and crawled into the lower bunk.

After a while, Paulie said, "I wish Mom and Dad didn't have to travel so much."

Steff tried to be cheerful. It was hard in the dark. She said, "When our family business gets going, they won't have to."

"I wish Mom could stay home—I mean, really home all the time—like she used to."

"She can't. She's got to help Dad. If they don't go places and tell people how good our stuff is, no one will buy it."

"I wish Dad had never been laid off from his job."

"Well, he was. And he couldn't find another one."

Paulie sighed. "I know."

"Don't forget to say your prayers."

"OK. But, Steff," Paulie whispered, "where do you think the cat is now?"

"Far away." Steff closed her eyes. Suppose a cat had not knocked over the soda cans? Suppose Aunt Opal was right, and a prowler had been looking in the back door?

3

past-due bill

The next morning, Steff made a space on the kitchen table for her cereal bowl. She made another space for Paulie's.

Choosing from all those boxes of cereal was fun.

But something had to be done about Aunt Opal's house. Every room was packed full of stuff.

Steff remembered the attic on the second floor. Perhaps she and Aunt Opal could put some things there.

She ran up to the attic.

It was cluttered, too.

Aunt Opal called, "Girls, I'm leaving now."

Steff hurried down to the living room.

Aunt Opal stood before a mirror. She put a floppy straw hat over the puff of gray hair on top of her head.

Steff said, "You're going someplace? I thought maybe we could . . . that is, maybe I could help you with the housework."

"Goodness, I dusted yesterday. What's there to do? It's nearly ten o'clock. Time for me to go uptown. I go uptown every day."

Aunt Opal hung her black pocketbook over her arm. She stepped out on the front porch and said, "If you go to the beach, lock the door. The key is under a flowerpot."

The beach was about two blocks away.

Aunt Opal walked the other direction.

Steff remembered that Aunt Opal's uptown was a street with lots of small shops.

Steff found a broom to sweep the front porch.

One of the posts that held up the roof wiggled when Steff hit it with the broom. Tiny crumbs, like sawdust, floated to the floor. Aunt Opal's house was old.

Paulie put on her swimsuit. "Let's go to the beach."

"Later," Steff said. "I have to start getting this place in order."

"I want to go to the beach."

"Quit nagging."

In the living room, Steff picked up some papers from the floor. "Must be mail." One sheet was falling out of its envelope. "Look at this."

Paulie stood on tiptoe to see. She said, "It's not polite to read other people's mail."

"It's a bill from the electric company."

Paulie pointed. "What's that red writing?"

"Wow!" Steff cried. "This bill is *past due*. It should have been paid a long time ago. Maybe the electric company will turn off the power."

"You mean the lights won't work?"

"Maybe," Steff said.

Paulie said, "Aunt Opal probably didn't pay the bill because it was lost."

Steff said, "Maybe we should tell her we found it."

"*You* found it. You were poking your nose in her mail."

"I was not!" Steff marched to the table where Aunt Opal kept her Bible. She put the electric company bill near the Bible and said, "Aunt Opal is sure to see it there."

Steff looked around the room. The keys on the old piano were yellow. A crack ran across one corner of the mirror.

Steff said, "Maybe Aunt Opal didn't lose that electric bill. Maybe she doesn't have enough money to pay it."

4

Stranger on the Porch

Steff and Paulie walked to the beach.

"Perhaps Aunt Opal can't keep track of her money very well," Steff said. "I wonder if she would want me to set up a budget for her."

Paulie said, "I hate it when you make budgets."

Steff didn't like that answer.

She told Paulie sternly, "Mom said you have to stay near the lifeguard."

"You, too!" Paulie ran toward the water.

Steff knew the rules. Neither of them could go in water higher than their knees. And the waves couldn't splash higher than their stomachs.

She threw down her stuff and ran, too.

There were lots of people sprawled over the beach. Steff ran between them.

She passed Paulie.

Then Steff's foot caught on something. She tripped and fell. Her chin dug a long ditch in the sand. She sat up and spit sand out of her mouth.

"Hey!" cried someone behind her.

A boy about Steff's age lay on his stomach. "You should look where you're going," he grumbled.

Steff grumbled back, "You should not take up the whole beach."

He shook sand from a magazine. A page dropped out.

Steff held her head high and walked away.

Paulie caught up. She said, "You kicked that boy's magazine so hard it tore. I saw a picture of a cross on it."

"I didn't kick it. Besides, he seems like a grouch to me."

"It sure looked like you kicked it."

The water was cold on Steff's knees.

She said, "Let's go back to Aunt Opal's house."

"But we just got here," Paulie said. "You're mad because you fell down and looked silly."

"I did not look silly. But I do have to organize that house."

Steff did not see the boy on the beach as they left.

When they reached Aunt Opal's house, both girls stopped out on the sidewalk.

A man stood on the front porch.

He was big. He wore a brown shirt and long brown pants. He was not dressed for a trip to the beach.

Steff thought about walking on past the house.

But it was too late. The man saw the girls.

He came down the steps toward them.

Paulie gasped and moved behind Steff.

Steff stood still and tried not to stare at the man's face. It was hard not to.

An ugly red scar ran across one cheek.

5

Message for Aunt Opal

The man came out to the sidewalk.

Now Steff could see lots of red freckles on his cheek.

The scar zigzagged from freckle to freckle. The freckles made the scar look bigger than it really was.

The man asked, "Do you girls know the woman who lives here?"

Steff nodded. She had never seen anyone with a dot-to-dot puzzle on his cheek.

"My name is Mr. Zacker. When will she be back?"

Steff shrugged.

Mr. Zacker's thick eyebrows wrinkled in a frown. He said, "Please tell her I'll stop by another time. I want to talk with her. I want to rent a room."

The girls backed out of the way.

Mr. Zacker walked by them and went down the street.

They watched him turn the corner. Then, they dashed to the front porch and began to giggle.

"He wants to pay money to stay here!" Steff dropped into a chair and threw up her hands. "In *this* house?"

Paulie leaned over the railing and screeched to the empty sidewalk, "Sorry, Mister. All the rooms in this house are full." She laughed. "Very full!"

"I know what, Paulie!" Steff cried. "We could build an extra floor in the attic. We could build it on top of other things. Up near the ceiling."

Paulie bent over and walked like a monkey.

"Of course, Mr. Zacker couldn't stand up in his room."

They laughed until Paulie said, "I'm hungry."

In the kitchen, Steff counted nineteen cans of black bean soup. Black bean soup didn't sound good. She found peanut butter and bread.

After lunch, Steff opened the cabinet under the sink. Out fell three bottles of soap for washing dishes. Each bottle was almost empty.

She emptied all the soap into one bottle.

"Should you be bothering things?" Paulie asked.

"I'm not bothering things. I'm *organizing* things."

Steff worked for a long time. Then she plopped on the floor and drank a soda.

Aunt Opal came home. She carried a shopping bag and her black pocketbook. She also carried a large, lumpy bundle wrapped in brown paper.

Aunt Opal took three jars from her shopping bag. "You girls like fig marmalade? It's good on toast."

Paulie screwed up her face.

"Dee-lish!" Aunt Opal put two jars into a cabinet. There wasn't room for the third. She set it on top of the toaster. "We'll just open a jar for supper."

Steff told her, "Mom said we should help with the housework. I already started to straighten things up."

"That's nice." Aunt Opal pulled two rolls of paper towels from her bag. "Got a good price on these."

She gave them to Paulie. "Put them away, will you, dear?"

"Where?" asked Paulie.

"Oh, wherever you like," answered Aunt Opal.

Paulie held the rolls of paper towels for a while.

Then she leaned down and rolled them under the kitchen table.

Aunt Opal asked, "Anybody hungry? How about a bowl of yummy black bean soup?"

Paulie screwed up her face again.

Steff said, "Thank you, but we just ate lunch."

Aunt Opal said, "Then I'll have a snack.

Steff, hand me an apple from the back porch."

On the back porch, Steff could see into a window in the house next door. That house was newer than Aunt Opal's.

She saw a boy walk through the room. It was the grouchy boy from the beach. He was their neighbor!

Then Steff remembered she had not told Aunt Opal about the visitor with the dot-to-dot puzzle on his face.

"Aunt Opal, a man was here today. He wants to rent a room in your house."

Aunt Opal cleared off a chair. She sat down.

"Hrmmph! I don't want to rent a room to anybody. If I did, I'd put up a sign. Why would he want to rent from me?"

thieves and moths

The next morning was Sunday. The girls put on flowered dresses. Aunt Opal wore a black dress and a black hat.

Steff and Paulie followed her uptown. They passed many little stores.

Aunt Opal stopped at a doorway next to a bicycle shop. A sign read *Bible Community Church.*

"This looks like a store," said Paulie.

"It used to be," Aunt Opal told her.

Steff peered in the window. Rows of folding

chairs sat on a bare floor.

Aunt Opal said, "Remember, Christ's church is not a building."

The preacher talked about treasures on earth. He talked about treasures in heaven. He talked about thieves that steal things and about moths that destroy things.

Everyone turned to Matthew 6. "Do not store up for yourselves treasures on earth," the preacher read.

Steff thought about that. Aunt Opal stored up lots of stuff. She had stored up fourteen bottles of soy sauce in a turkey roaster.

Then Steff saw the boy from the beach.

Paulie had said his magazine had a picture of a cross. Maybe it was a Bible story. Steff hoped she hadn't torn it too badly.

That afternoon, a man came to Aunt Opal's house.

She stood at the front door and talked with him. She told him, "I don't have a room for rent."

Paulie watched out the window as he walked away. She said, "That's Mr. Zacker, the man who came yesterday."

"Who is he?" Steff asked.

"He *says* he's a missionary." Aunt Opal frowned. "But I wonder if he is."

A shiver rippled down Steff's back.

"He *says* he heard that I might have a room to rent. Hrmmph! I think he's heard about a certain item that I have."

"A certain item?" Steff asked.

"Come with me, girls," said Aunt Opal. "I want you to see something."

Steff and Paulie scrambled after her. She led the way up the stairs into the attic.

There, they zigged and zagged around stuff until they came to an old desk.

Aunt Opal reached under it and brought out a cardboard box. The box was the right size to hold a doll. A big doll.

"I want you to see my treasure," she said.

She glanced around the attic as if making sure no one else lurked in the corners.

She tapped the box softly with one finger. "There is only one treasure in this house—only one thing worth stealing. Of course, I don't leave it under this desk all the time. I move it to a new hiding place often, and I wrap it in different ways—to fool anyone who might come poking around."

"Is that box full of money?" Paulie asked.

"Money? I should say not." Aunt Opal took off the lid. "Look. Here is my treasure."

Steff and Paulie leaned over the box.

Paulie said politely, "Oh. That's nice."

It didn't look like much of a treasure to Steff either.

It was just a big wooden clock with fancy numbers.

But it must be worth a lot of money if Aunt Opal said it was a treasure.

7

footsteps in the kitchen

The next morning, Aunt Opal left to go up-town.

Steff worked hard sorting and moving things. Paulie helped her.

After lunch, they carried armloads of stuff to the alley behind the house. They filled Aunt Opal's trash cans, but there was more to throw away.

Steff saw two empty cans in the alley. "These must belong to the house next door.

Let's ask if we can use one."

The boy they had met on the beach lived in that house. Steff hoped he wasn't angry with her.

When he opened the door, Steff said, "I'm sorry I ran over you at the beach."

The boy shrugged and said, "Okay." His name was Tim. He helped move the rest of the stuff to the alley.

Steff decided Tim wasn't grouchy after all.

An older boy came down the alley.

He carried a surfboard. His hair was almost white.

"What you got there?" he asked.

"Junk," Tim said.

Steff had never known a surfer. He seemed okay. He didn't hang around long.

Steff went back to sorting things.

But Paulie kept asking, "When can we go to the beach?"

Finally, Steff said, "Okay," and put on her swimsuit.

When they got to the beach, Tim was there digging in wet sand.

"He's making a whale," Paulie said. "Want to ask if we can help?"

"I guess so," Steff said.

They couldn't go in the water past their knees anyway.

Later, Steff and Paulie walked back to Aunt Opal's house.

Aunt Opal came home from uptown. She carried another large, lumpy package.

Steff started to ask Aunt Opal about the package, but just then Tim knocked on the door. He wanted Steff and Paulie to play a board game on the front porch.

Steff said, "Sure. But don't lean on that post." She pointed to the wiggly one with sawdust around it.

"Termites," said Tim.

That night when it got dark, Steff flipped a light switch. No lights came on.

Aunt Opal said, "I wonder if the power plant is having a problem."

"It's not that," Paulie said. "Steff saw—"

Steff broke in, "I happened to see an envelope from the electric company. It was on the floor. I put it on the table by your Bible."

"Oh, dear," said Aunt Opal. "I hope I didn't throw it away."

She tried the light switch herself. "I suppose it could have been the bill."

They all went to bed early.

Sometime in the night Steff woke up. She heard a noise.

Shwussh, shwussh.

The noise came from the kitchen. Maybe it was footsteps. Maybe Aunt Opal was in the kitchen.

THUNK!

That was not Aunt Opal. She wouldn't bump into things.

Steff thought she should go to her aunt's bedroom and wake her. But she didn't want to get out of bed.

While she was still thinking about it, a shriek rang out. It sounded like Aunt Opal.

Loud noises burst from the kitchen. *CRASH-BANG! THUMP!*

Paulie woke up and screamed.

The back door slammed.

Paulie swung down from the top bunk and jumped in with Steff.

They lay perfectly still. The house grew quiet.

A light switch snapped softly. No lights came on. It snapped again.

"Hrmmph!"

Steff sat up in bed. "Aunt Opal, is that you?"

A circle of light danced into the bedroom. It danced its way to the bunk beds.

"Don't worry, girls." Aunt Opal waved a flashlight. "The prowler struck again. But he's gone now. And he didn't find the treasure."

accident in the attic

Two police officers came the next morning. They said maybe Aunt Opal had forgotten to lock the back door.

Aunt Opal said they were probably right.

After the police officers left, Aunt Opal picked up her black pocketbook.

On the way out the door, she said, "I think I'll pay the electric bill while I'm uptown."

Steff climbed the stairs to the attic. It was a mess. She sighed and began to work.

She tossed empty boxes down the stairs and yelled to Paulie, "Put those in the trash."

She found a ragged, tattered white blanket. She rolled it down the stairs like a ball of string. "For the trash!"

Not everything was trash.

"Paulie," Steff called. "Guess what I see—a bunch of shopping bags filled with your yarn!"

Paulie groaned.

Steff found picture frames, and books, and a fancy velvet cape with only one hole.

Paulie came upstairs. She put on the cape and pretended to pour tea from a cracked teapot.

"I know what," Steff told her. "We'll have a yard sale. We can sell this good stuff and put the money in Aunt Opal's cookie jar."

A rubber boot stuck out of a box on a high shelf. Steff climbed on a trunk to reach it.

The box was heavy.

Steff tugged. She tugged harder.

The box moved. Steff lost her balance. She fell off the trunk and down to the floor.

"Ouch!" she cried.

"Are you hurt?" asked Paulie.

"Ouch, ouch!" Steff moved a little. "I hurt, but I guess I'm not *hurt* hurt."

Something lumpy was under her—something lumpy wrapped in brown paper.

Paulie peeked inside the brown paper. "Oh no! Look what you did."

There lay the clock. It was crushed, with shattered glass and twisted hands.

Paulie said, "I thought Aunt Opal's clock was in a box."

"Remember? She moves it around and changes the way it's wrapped. She probably took her clock from the box, wrapped it in this brown paper, and put it in this new hiding place."

"So a prowler wouldn't find it," Paulie said. "But you sure did!"

They folded the brown paper around the pieces and carried them down to the back porch.

"Look for glue," said Steff.

They found four bottles. Steff used most of one bottle on the clock. It didn't help.

"Hi!" came a cheerful voice.

Steff jumped in front of the broken clock to hide it.

It was only Tim.

Paulie told him, "Steff broke Aunt Opal's clock. It's a treasure."

"Huh?" Tim looked at the clock. "Throw it in the trash."

Steff squeezed the glue bottle harder.

Tim said, "You can't fix that. Buy your aunt another."

"Are you kidding?" Steff said. "This is a one-of-a-kind clock."

"Oh yeah?" Tim rolled his eyes. "Come with me—and bring money."

They walked uptown. Steff kept watching for Aunt Opal. They ducked into a little shop.

In one room was a clock that looked just like Aunt Opal's. In fact, there were dozens of clocks that looked like Aunt Opal's.

Tim said, "Buy one. They don't cost much."

Paulie told him. "Steff never wants to spend her money. She's saving for a planner book."

"Not just a planner book," Steff corrected her. "It's an entire planning *system*."

She didn't have enough money to buy a planning system anyway. But someday she would.

Then she'd really get things organized.

They bought the clock.

Steff took the new clock to Aunt Opal's attic. She wrapped it in the brown paper and left it on the floor by the trunk.

Paulie watched. "Is it okay if you don't tell Aunt Opal you broke her clock?"

Steff said, "Probably. That store had dozens of clocks. So the one I broke wasn't a treasure after all. I guess Aunt Opal just thought it was."

9

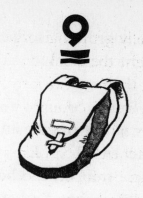

Yard Sale

The next morning, Aunt Opal put on her hat to go uptown.

Steff said, "We found an old velvet cape with a hole in it."

"Oh, my. Is that still around?"

"Can we try to sell it?" Steff asked.

"Hrmmph! I suppose so. I don't need a velvet cape."

Steff said, "Maybe Paulie and I can sell more old stuff you don't need. Is that OK?"

Aunt Opal started out the front door.

Steff called after her, "Is that OK?"

Aunt Opal waved from the sidewalk. "I suppose so."

Steff and Paulie brought the cape and a bunch of other stuff from the attic. They made a sign that read YARD SALE.

Many people stopped and bought things.

The yarn was a good seller. One woman bought all of it.

Paulie's chin dropped in surprise. Steff had to tell her not to stare.

Later, Steff and Paulie slipped the money into Aunt Opal's chicken cookie jar.

Their first yard sale was such a success that they held another the next day. Then another. And another.

They held them in the mornings after Aunt Opal left to go uptown.

"Are you sure it's okay to do this?" Paulie asked Steff.

"Aunt Opal said to sell stuff, didn't she?" Steff answered.

Each morning, Steff and Paulie sorted things and put up the yard sale sign.

Each afternoon, they put the money in Aunt Opal's chicken cookie jar.

Then they went to the beach.

Most mornings, Tim helped. Some afternoons, he went to the beach, too.

Most mornings, the blond surfer came. He never bought anything.

Most mornings, Mr. Zacker came. Sometimes he bought a little something.

One day, Steff was in the house. She had washed a tiny statue of a lady in a long dress. The lady's dress was chipped. Steff was pretty sure no one would buy it.

Paulie and Tim were working outside.

Steff looked out the window. The blond surfer was finally buying something. He handed Tim money.

Steff gasped. She dropped the statue. Now it was really chipped. She ran to the door.

Tim was giving the blond surfer a large, lumpy bundle.

"Hey!" Steff yelled. "That's not for sale."

The bundle with Aunt Opal's clock had gotten in the yard sale by mistake.

The surfer reached for the bundle. "I just bought it."

Tim held on. "Sorry." He returned the money.

The surfer spit on the sidewalk. Then he stomped away.

Steff took the bundle inside.

The clock wasn't a treasure. But Steff did not want to have to buy another to replace this one.

10

Mr. Zacker's book

Some evenings, Mr. Zacker visited. He sat on the front porch and drank lemonade with Aunt Opal.

Aunt Opal didn't seem worried about him anymore.

He told stories about being a missionary in Africa. That was where he fell down a cliff and got his scar.

Steff and Paulie were getting used to seeing the dot-to-dot puzzle on his cheek.

But they still thought he was trying to steal the treasure.

"Of course, there really isn't any treasure," Steff reminded Paulie.

One evening, Mr. Zacker brought a book to show Aunt Opal.

Suddenly, Aunt Opal clapped her hands. "Girls! Here is a picture of my clock in Mr. Zacker's book."

Steff got a funny feeling in her stomach.

"See that mark just below the clock's face?" Aunt Opal told the girls. "It looks a little like a lion. My clock has that mark, too."

Steff couldn't believe she was seeing Aunt Opal's clock in a book.

"Oh. It *was* a real treasure," Paulie said. "We thought. . . ."

Steff jabbed her sister hard.

Steff went inside and hurried up to the attic. She pulled out the clock she had bought at the shop to replace the broken one. There was no lion mark on this one.

Steff sank down against the old trunk. Aunt Opal's lion clock *had* been a real treasure. And Steff had broken it!

But Aunt Opal didn't know. She thought

her clock was still safely hidden in the house.

So did Mr. Zacker.

That night, the girls were getting ready for bed.

Paulie said, "You have to tell Aunt Opal you broke her treasure."

"It's too late tonight," Steff said.

"Are you going to tell Mom about it the next time she calls us?"

"Maybe."

In the morning, Paulie said again, "You have to tell Aunt Opal you broke her treasure."

"Later. It's time to go to church."

Tim came. Paulie told him about the treasure.

Tim looked at Steff. "You have to tell your aunt you broke her treasure."

"I will. I will. Leave me alone!"

On the way to church, Steff thought, *Maybe I don't have to tell Aunt Opal I broke her clock. When she finds out it is gone, she will think the prowler came and stole it.*

In church, the preacher talked about treasures again.

Steff squirmed. She told herself that Aunt Opal shouldn't lay up so many treasures. Aunt Opal should not care about a clock, even if it had a lion mark on it.

Steff opened her Bible to Matthew and read the part about treasures. She read about moths.

Steff was a kind of moth. She had destroyed Aunt Opal's treasure.

When they got home from church, Aunt Opal sat in her rocking chair. She rocked and rocked and didn't bump into anything.

"My," Aunt Opal said, "this room seems larger than it once did."

Paulie said, "That's because we sold—"

"Aunt Opal," Steff said quickly, "I have something important to tell you."

Aunt Opal was still admiring the living room. "It's brighter, too."

"Aunt Opal," Steff said. "I broke your treasure."

Aunt Opal stopped rocking. "You what?"

"I broke your treasure. I'm sorry. It was an accident. I was trying to organize your house."

Aunt Opal got up. "Come with me. You, too, Paulie."

They followed Aunt Opal into her bedroom. She pulled a bundle wrapped in white cloth from under the bed. Aunt Opal unrolled the bundle.

Steff gasped.

Paulie scrambled closer.

There in the soft white cloth was a clock. Steff looked carefully. Below the clock face was a lion mark.

"I don't understand," Steff said. "Your clock was in the attic. I fell on it and broke it."

"Hrmmph!" Aunt Opal wrapped the white cloth around the treasure and put it back under the bed. "You must have broken a fake clock. I keep fake clocks around to fool people who might come to steal the real clock."

"It fooled Steff," Paulie said.

Steff frowned at her.

Aunt Opal said, "A thief couldn't tell which is a fake, and which is the real treasure."

She went to the closet and took out a large bag. In it was a clock just like the one Steff had

bought. It did not have a lion mark.

"I buy them uptown," Aunt Opal said.

Aunt Opal had even hidden a fake clock under the round table on the front porch. The tablecloth hung to the floor and covered it.

That night in bed, Steff whispered to Paulie, "I'm glad I told Aunt Opal about breaking the clock. I'm even more glad that the one I broke was not a treasure."

Paulie answered softly, "But Mr. Zacker knows there is a treasure. What if he tries to steal it?"

the white bundle

The next afternoon, Steff and Paulie were coming from the beach.

Tim's mother called, "I have a plate of cookies for you girls and your aunt."

Paulie went to get them.

Steff put their beach stuff on the front porch. She found the house key under a flowerpot.

But the door was not locked. Steff thought she had locked it. Maybe Aunt Opal had come home early.

Steff walked into the living room.

She heard footsteps coming down the stairs from the attic.

A weird feeling made Steff back away. She backed toward the front door. She backed all the way out to the front porch.

The footsteps turned into a loud clatter. Someone rushed through the front door and started down the porch steps.

Steff saw who it was. She tried to be brave. She yelled, "Hey!"

It was the blond surfer.

He turned around. In his arms, he carried a large, lumpy bundle wrapped in white cloth.

He walked toward Steff. There was sweat on his face. His blue eyes darted here and there.

Steff looked at the white bundle. She tried to think of something to say. "Th-the next yard sale is tomorrow."

"I bought this at the sale this morning," the surfer said. "Your sister sold it to me."

That was not true. Steff knew when Paulie sold something because Paulie always hopped around and laughed.

The surfer's voice sounded like a snarl from a mean dog. "I was carrying my board this morning. So your sister put this in the house for me to get later."

He opened the bundle a little. "See?"

Steff moved as close as she dared.

Inside the bundle was a clock. She saw the face. Then she saw something else.

Just below the clock's face was the lion mark.

This was Aunt Opal's treasure! The surfer was taking it away.

"Let me see it better." Steff tried not to sound scared.

The surfer grinned a little. He held the clock out to Steff. He even let her hold it.

What could Steff do?

She couldn't run out to the yard. The surfer stood in the way.

She couldn't run into the house either. If she did, he would come after her and take the clock.

The surfer was a thief. He was stealing Aunt Opal's treasure.

And Steff didn't know how to stop him.

12

cookie spill

Just then, Paulie came skipping from Tim's house.

"Look at all the cookies!" She held up a paper plate. "Chocolate chip!"

The surfer turned toward her.

Tim was coming behind Paulie. Paulie saw the surfer and stopped. Tim bumped into her and knocked her down.

She screamed.

The plate flew high into the air. Cookies tumbled out and spilled everywhere.

Tim tripped over Paulie and fell down on top of her and the cookies.

The surfer laughed and kept watching them.

Steff had an idea.

The lion clock was in her arms. She dropped to the porch floor.

The tablecloth on the round table hung to the floor. She reached under the tablecloth and felt around. She remembered Aunt Opal had hidden a fake clock there.

Steff's fingers touched something. She yanked it out.

It was the fake clock. Quickly, Steff pushed the real clock under the tablecloth.

Then, she shoved the fake clock across the floor toward the surfer's feet.

He turned and saw it sliding toward him. He bent to grab it. He moved so quickly that he knocked against the post with the sawdust.

The post creaked and wobbled sideways. Sawdust puffed up.

The roof began to groan. The post came crashing down.

It fell right across the clock on the floor.

The post smashed the clock. The clock was as flat as the cookies Paulie had dropped.

The surfer scrambled to his feet. "You broke it!" he cried. He said more things, too—mean things.

Then he ran out of the yard and down the sidewalk.

He ran by a man and a woman coming into the yard.

The woman was Aunt Opal.

"I've brought someone from the museum to see my clock," she said. She looked at the sagging porch roof. "Oh, dear. Did we have an earthquake?"

Steff told Aunt Opal what happened.

The man from the museum said, "That blond fellow once worked at the museum. He would know that your clock is valuable."

"Aha," said Aunt Opal. "Now we know who the prowler was."

Steff chuckled. "He thinks the valuable clock is broken. He didn't see me push the one with the lion mark under the table."

The man looked at the lion clock carefully and talked with Aunt Opal. Then he left.

Aunt Opal told the girls and Tim, "The people at the museum will buy my clock. They will give me a lot of money for it. In the museum, the clock will be safe, and everyone can see it."

"Will the museum pay enough money to fix the porch?" asked Paulie.

Aunt Opal nodded.

Mr. Zacker came.

They told him the story.

"Now Aunt Opal can fix the porch," said Paulie.

"I'll do more than that," Aunt Opal said. "Mr. Zacker and I have been talking. I have decided to fix up some of my rooms and rent them out."

Mr. Zacker said, "Missionaries sometimes come here to the beach for a rest. They need a place to stay that is not expensive."

Paulie said, "But, Aunt Opal, you have a lot of stuff in every room."

"Too much stuff. I don't mind getting rid of it. Besides, I like the way the house looks now that you girls have been clearing things out."

Steff gulped. "I thought you were storing up treasures."

"Hrmmph! Why would I do that? Yes, the clock is a treasure. But it's an earthly treasure. Nothing I have is as important to me as my treasure in heaven."

Then Aunt Opal grinned at Steff. "There will also be enough money to buy that planner you want so badly."

"A real planning system!" cried Steff. "Oh, thank you!"

Then Steff began to wonder. Maybe she cared too much about having a planner. She was always thinking what she would do with it.

Would a planner become Steff's most important treasure?

"Aunt Opal," she said. "Do you mind if we wait a while to buy the planner?"

"Huh?" cried Paulie.

Aunt Opal asked, "Have you changed your mind about it?"

Steff shook her head. "No. I just want to be sure my treasure in heaven is always going to be the most important treasure I have."

Aunt Opal's eyes got shiny. She cleared her throat.

Then she said, "I think Mr. Zacker would like a cookie."

They all went into the kitchen. Aunt Opal took the lid off the chicken cookie jar.

"Hrmmph!" she said. "Tim, does your mother have any more cookies? My cookie jar is full of money."

Paulie giggled. She poked Steff.

Steff giggled. She poked Paulie.

They both ran after Tim to help him bring the cookies.

the end

Series for Young Readers*
From Bethany House Publishers

The Adventures of Callie Ann
by Shannon Mason Leppard

Readers will giggle their way through the true-to-life escapades of Callie Ann Davies and her many North Carolina friends.

AstroKids™
by Robert Elmer

Space scooters? Floating robots? Jupiter ice cream? Blast into the future for out-of-this-world, zero-gravity fun with the AstroKids on space station *CLEO-7*.

Backpack Mysteries
by Mary Carpenter Reid

This excitement-filled mystery series follows the mishaps and adventures of Steff and Paulie Larson as they strive to help often-eccentric relatives crack their toughest cases.

The Cul-de-sac Kids
by Beverly Lewis

Each story in this lighthearted series features the hilarious antics and predicaments of nine endearing boys and girls who live on Blossom Hill Lane.

Janette Oke's Animal Friends
by Janette Oke

Endearing creatures from the farm, forest, and zoo discover their place in God's world through various struggles, mishaps, and adventures.

Ruby Slippers School
by Stacy Towle Morgan

Join the fun as home-schoolers Hope and Annie Brown visit fascinating countries and meet inspiring Christians from around the world!

Three Cousins Detective Club®
by Elspeth Campbell Murphy

Famous detective cousins Timothy, Titus, and Sarah-Jane learn compelling Scripture-based truths while finding—and solving—intriguing mysteries.

*(ages 7–10)